Dragon Eggs Book 3

Dragon's First Christmas

Emily Martha Sorensen

Also by Emily Martha Sorensen

Books:

Black Magic Academy
The Keeper and the Rulership
The Fires of the Rulership
Worlds of Wonder
Tabby, Tabby, Burning Bright

Dragon Eggs:

Dragon's Egg
Dragon's Hope

Fairy Senses:

Fairy Eyeglasses
Fairy Compass
Fairy Earmuffs
Fairy Barometer
Fairy Pox
Fairy Slippers
Fairy Lunchbox

Comics:

A Magical Roommate
To Prevent World Peace

Dragon Eggs Book #3: Dragon's First Christmas
Copyright © 2016 by Emily Martha Sorensen
Cover art by Eva Urbaníková

ISBN-13: 978-1-949607-04-8
ISBN-10: 1-949607-04-6

http://www.emilymarthasorensen.com

For Ann Keeran,
beta-reader and typo-finder extraordinaire.

For Meredith Dixon,
whose knowledge of historical accuracy
far surpasses my own.

CHAPTER 1
Charred

A scaly head poked up under Rose's toes, which were cold from hanging out of the blankets at the end of the bed.

The tree was hot and bright. Could he play with it?

"We're not lighting the candles before Christmas Eve," Henry murmured from beside her. "Virgil, go back to sleep."

The tree was hot and bright now. Virgil had sneezed, and the tree was hot and bright. Could he play with it?

Rose's eyes flew open.

"You set it on *fire?!*" Henry shouted.

It was hot and bright. Virgil had made it pretty. Could he —

Both of them were already scrambling out of bed and moving. Henry pounded down the hallway ahead of her, so Rose swerved into the bathroom to seize a towel and dunk it in the toilet. Drenched towel in hand, she raced after him.

The bottom of the Christmas tree was wreathed in flames. Henry was beating it out with a cushion, without much success. A spark caught the wick of a candle that had fallen askew from the beating, and fire licked up the branch it was perched on.

Rose joined in with the wet towel. Each time she thought she'd caught it all, another lick of flame curled up, and she had to beat back branch after branch after branch.

At last, just as she was thinking the last sparks were finally gone, the charred tree fell over with a resounding crash.

Henry waited, poised, blackened cushion in hand.

Rose's heart hammered as she held the soaked, soot-covered towel.

"I think it's out," Henry said with relief.

Virgil's parents had been hitting the tree, and now it wasn't pretty anymore. Why was it on the floor?

Henry spun around and glared at the little dragon who was moving down the hallway.

Virgil was half-rolling, half-crawling, using his tail for balance, as he was wont to do. His arms and legs were not yet strong enough to hold up his weight, but he still squirmed along at a rapid pace that any human two-month-old would envy. Their baby crawl-rolled closer, seeming completely oblivious to the danger he had just put them in.

The tree wasn't pretty anymore. Could he still play with it?

"You are not supposed to get out of bed without permission!" Henry roared. "Do you understand?!"

Virgil's tail whipped around his head, as if to hide him.

Virgil's father was angry. Virgil was sad. Virgil was very sad. Virgil was going to scream.

"No!" Rose said immediately, leaping to the little dragon. She ran her hand along his head to comfort him. "No, Virgil. No screaming. Remember?"

Virgil was sad! Virgil was very sad! Virgil was feeling better. The tree wasn't pretty anymore. Could he still play with it?

Without a word, Henry spun around and stalked into the kitchen. He came back with a broom and dustpan, which he used to start sweeping blackened needles and shattered ornaments off the carpet. His arms moved fiercely. Sweep. Sweep. Sweep.

It was bizarre that Rose was the one left comforting the baby. Usually Virgil preferred Henry, who was far more sympathetic and patient with him.

"There, there," Rose murmured, wondering if that would be at all sufficient. What did Henry usually say to prevent tantrumming?

Chapter 1: Charred

Sometimes she felt like they were doing just fine raising Virgil. Other times, the enormity of the task swept over her. This was one of those times. Here they were in 1920, millions of years after the rest of his species had gone extinct, two humans trying to care for a *Deinonychus antirrhopus* dragon baby. Despite the fact that they were doing it, sometimes it seemed impossible, or even ludicrous.

If they had been *Deinonychus* parents, they would have been far more equal to the task. If Virgil had not been the first, at least they could have benefited from other human parents' advice. But no, they were the only ones who could figure out what Virgil needed. And now — Rose's heart pounded as she thought of the danger they had just been in — they did not even know how to protect themselves, much less him.

She had thought that if more of the dragon eggs at the museum hatched, it would make their task easier. After all, there would be other parents in their situation to swap ideas with. But in some ways, the presence of Violet in the city only made things more difficult. Because Violet . . .

Virgil squirmed under her fingers, apparently catching her thoughts, as he did all too frequently when she least wanted him to. The tendency reminded her of her sisters' proclivity to eavesdrop on everything.

Virgil liked Violet. Could Virgil go to visit Violet? Her house had lots of interesting prey!

Henry slammed the trash can onto the floor beside him, then emptied the dustpan into it. "No, Virgil," he said sharply. "We are not going to reward you with a trip to the zoo for burning down the Christmas tree."

Virgil was disappointed. Virgil thought Violet was interesting. Could Virgil play with the tree?

"*No!*" Henry shouted.

Violet lived in the zoo. A place where they were determined their son must not end up. A place filled with well-meaning people who kept pressuring them to transfer Virgil to their care because they thought they could do better for him.

Perhaps, Rose thought grimly, staring at the charred remnants of their Christmas tree, *perhaps they were right.*

They couldn't allow this to happen again. It had been pure luck that nothing worse had happened. So what if the best thing for both them and Virgil would be . . .?

Rose stood, restlessly. She cradled Virgil in her arms and strode into the kitchen. The little dragon wriggled and nearly sunk his curved back claws into her arm, but she had grown deft at avoiding them.

She opened the door to the appliance that had once been an oven, but was now Virgil's bed. There was no longer gas connected to it, which made it impossible for them to cook their own food at home. They had been borrowing their neighbors' ovens for several weeks now, or else eating their food cold, ever since Virgil had figured out how to escape the bathtub they had originally used as his bed.

She placed the little dragon inside and shut the door until it rested against the curved piece of metal they had nailed to the inside of the door. It acted as a doorstop to keep it from closing entirely, so that there was always a crack for air to get in so that Virgil could breathe.

Virgil wriggled around, his tail thumping against the side, his claws scraping the floor. He was restless! He was tired! He didn't want to be in his bed! He wanted to be playing with the tree that wasn't pretty! He was angry! He was sleepy! Maybe he would take a nap.

Rose waited with bated breath, trying not to think of anything, as Virgil's thoughts settled down and he ceased to communicate. At last, when she was fairly certain he was asleep, she walked out of the kitchen, a deep weariness settling over her.

She worked with Henry in silence, cleaning up the shattered ornaments and singed pine needles. At last, when they were finished, they lifted up the tree together.

Unsurprisingly, the carpet underneath where the tree had stood was charred, and even the wood underneath was blackened in the spots it was visible through the holes in the carpet.

Chapter 1: Charred

"So much for hiding this from our landlord," Rose joked.

Henry did not laugh.

Rose sighed. It wasn't really funny. The man had been outraged when he'd seen what they'd done to the oven. They had not informed him that Virgil could breathe fire, primarily because they had been hoping it would not cause any issues. That decision now seemed stupid and naive.

When he saw what had happened to the carpet, there was no doubt that he would evict them. And rightly so, really. If Virgil could now escape from his bed and wander around the apartment while they were sleeping, this would happen again. And again. And again. Staying here was no longer safe.

"What now?" Henry asked.

Rose swallowed. "I have no idea," she said.

CHAPTER 2
Chasten

Unspeakable as the zoo was as an option, it seemed nevertheless like a good place to go to ask for advice. Central Park Zoo had been taking care of Violet for two months now — or three weeks, if you counted only the time after she had hatched.

Henry seemed ill at ease as they approached the enclosure where Violet was kept. He was always uncomfortable when they came here, no doubt because he was afraid his son would wind up an exhibit. In fact, the only reason Rose had managed to convince him to come here the first time had been the urgent necessity of the two dragons meeting.

"After all, you can't deny Virgil the only chance he might have to play with another child of his species," Rose had said.

"There are ten eggs left in the museum," Henry had retorted. "Chances are, there will be other dragons he can play with later."

"We can't *know* that," Rose had shot back. "And in the meantime, why would you deny him the chance to meet another *Deinonychus* when he has the opportunity? Do you really think that is what is best for him?"

Now, as they passed an elephant loaded down with a dozen school children who were shouting and laughing, Henry walked with his shoulders hunched and his arms tensed.

Perhaps it was the sight of the powerful lions and tigers trapped behind metal bars in small spaces. Perhaps it was the children, whose parents were strolling beside the elephant as a zoo keeper led it down the walkway. Perhaps it was the fact that their son would never have that opportunity, and would in fact be far more likely to wind up behind the bars of a cage.

They stopped at Violet's enclosure.

Virgil poked his head out of the pram they had been pushing him in.

He was very excited! He had burned down the tree, so his parents had brought him here to see Violet!

"This is *not a reward*," Henry growled.

Rose looked around for the zoo worker who had been assigned to Violet. Given the dragon's intelligence, rarity, and fire-breathing, the zoo had prudently assigned a keeper to stay in the area at all times that the zoo was open to prevent any danger towards incautious patrons . . . or harassment from them. Sure enough, there was a man in a tweed suit and bowler hat tossing food into the grizzly bear cage just a few cages down.

As Virgil shared his happy memories of the burning tree — to Henry's evident frustration — Rose parted from her husband and child to walk over to the zoo keeper.

"Good morning, Mr. Westchester," she said politely. "How are things at the zoo today?"

The man turned and moved to tip his hat, then seemed to recall that he had just been holding raw meat in that hand. "Quite good," he said. "Can't complain. And you?"

Abysmal, Rose wanted to say. *Yesterday, Virgil started a fire while we were asleep, and we have no idea how to stop him from doing it again.* But she didn't dare say that. Mr. Westchester was one of the many people at the zoo who had been pressuring them to move Virgil there.

"Preparing for Christmas," she said cautiously. "We have been thinking about building a new bed for Virgil, something far more contained, in case he starts getting strong enough to crawl out of bed while we're asleep. Have you any suggestions?"

"Steel bars," the man said bluntly, pointing back at Violet's cage. "An apartment building wasn't built for dragons. We keep nothing flammable near her with good reason."

Rose's fists tightened at her sides. She reminded herself that civility was a necessity.

"We will not be taking Virgil to the zoo to live," she said in as level a voice as she could manage. "He is here only to visit Violet, and *she* is only here on sufferance of her father's agreement."

"She is *not* here on sufferance of Mr. Jones," the zoo keeper said, looking annoyed. He pulled a cloth from the pockets of his worn tweed pants and wiped his hands with it. "She is here by the permission of Director Campbell of the American Museum of Natural History, who owns all twelve of the dragon eggs. Including the one *he* hatched from."

The man jabbed his finger in the direction of the dragon cage, where Henry was lifting Virgil up to the bars so that he could watch Violet's tail swishing back and forth.

Heat swept across Rose's face in burning fury. That was a sore subject, one that she and Henry never mentioned, but which haunted her dreams at night. At any time, the director of the museum could take their son away, and they would have no legal recourse to get him back.

Which is wrong, Rose thought, her fists tightening. *Dragons are people, and people should not be legally held as property. There was a war to that effect last century!*

She had a long-term goal for Virgil, though she had not spoken of it to anyone. She would see to it that he would be legally recognized and given all the same rights as a human. He had been born into a world in which dragons were extinct, but she would not allow that to rob him of the rights he would have had if he had hatched in the Cretaceous Period.

Further reaching than that, she had a goal to see *Deinonychus antirrhopus* make a resurgence as a species. That was one of the reasons Rose had wanted Virgil to get to know Violet: she might well be the only female of his species he would have the opportunity to meet.

Rose could not force the two to marry, of course, nor would she wish to. But she could certainly see to it that they knew each other very well by the time they were adults.

Of course, seeing as they were both hatchlings right now, that sort of thinking was highly premature. But Rose had never been one to disregard the far future in her planning. She had decided at nine years old that she would become a paleontologist, and she had not changed her mind since.

The only thing that Virgil had changed was that, where once she had had one goal, now she had three.

Rose continued to stare at the zoo keeper in frosty silence.

The man looked a trifle uncomfortable. He moved away from her to walk over to Violet's cage, where a crowd of onlookers had been gathering.

"Can I pet the dragon, too?" a woman asked eagerly, crowding in and reaching out her hand.

"Didn't know there was more than one," a man said.

"Of course there is, didn't you read the news?" another man said impatiently. "This is the man who studies dragons and is raising one."

Rose's chest swelled with indignation. *I'M the one who's studying paleontology, not Henry!*

"No," Henry said, swatting the reaching hands away. "No, you can't pet him. No. No. No. *Stop it!*"

Virgil's claws dug into the front of Henry's shirt. He didn't like these hands. These hands were scary. He would make these hands go away.

Virgil started making snorting noises.

"Get back!" Henry shouted. "Get back right now!"

The crowd parted as he shoved them, and Virgil let loose a tiny spark. It danced briefly in the air, then disappeared.

Rose breathed a sigh of relief.

Virgil's tail wriggled as his head turned to face Violet.

Why was Violet sleeping? Virgil didn't want her to be sleeping. Virgil wanted her to wake up. He would wake her up with one of her memories she had shared with him.

"No!" Rose shouted, but she was too late.

A vision of terror and desolation gripped her mind. Her parents were gone. All the adults were gone. Only the eggs remained, screaming and screaming with nobody coming to claim them. No one would ever claim them. They would never hatch. *She* would never hatch. There was absolute despair.

Rose sucked in her breath as she returned to herself, and the tiny blue dragon within the cage twitched. Her eyes opened. Her claws scrambled against the cement beneath her. Then she opened her mouth and screamed.

The crowd shouted and covered their ears as the high-pitched shriek reverberated endlessly, and loudly.

Virgil was glad Violet had woken up! Now they could play together!

The terrible scream stopped.

The little blue dragon looked up. Piteousness emanated from her.

Was Violet not alone now? Had Violet just been dreaming?

Henry rapped Virgil sharply on the nose. "You do not wake people up by giving them nightmares! That is not acceptable!"

Virgil was sorry. Virgil hadn't meant to make Violet sad.

Violet was better. Violet was sleepy. Violet was tired. Maybe Violet would sleep again.

Virgil didn't want her to sleep. Virgil wanted her to wake up.

The little blue dragon's head drooped, and her tail curled back around her again.

No! Virgil would wake her up again, so she would play. No! Why was his father walking away? Violet should play!

"This was a bad idea," Henry said, walking over to Rose. "We can go somewhere else to ask for advice."

Where? Rose wondered.

But she didn't object. Henry was right. She should not have expected help to be forthcoming here.

Their son's tail writhed as they tucked him back into the pram.

Virgil was very upset! Violet should play!

Chapter 3
Challenge

The American Museum of Natural History was where they had met Virgil, and it was the one other place Rose could think of where there might be someone with helpful insights on baby dragons.

Someone in particular, and it wasn't Director Campbell.

Mr. Teedle, the curator of the dragon collection, was in the Research Library on the fourth floor. It was locked because it was not open to the public, but Rose found a staff member to open it for her.

As the door opened, Rose maneuvered the pram to push it through.

"What's that?" Mr. Teedle looked up from the table where he had been carefully paging through a book. "We're not open to the public right now. The hours are two pm to five thir—" He stopped, recognizing her. "Oh, Miss Palmer. To what do I owe the pleasure?"

"Mrs. Wainscott," Henry corrected him, coming in after Rose.

"Oh. Yes." Mr. Teedle coughed. "Please do forgive me."

"It's quite all right," Rose said. "I often forget that myself."

Mr. Teedle ran his hand down the slick surface of his greying hair. "And I see you have brought Virgil. Is he . . . ah . . . not likely to burn the reference materials in here?"

"He's asleep," Henry said. "He tired himself out throwing a fit on the way over here."

"Thank heavens," Mr. Teedle said, breathing a sigh of relief. "This is not a room where a firebreathing infant ought to be, you realize."

Henry's smile grew strained, and Rose recognized that his patience had frayed considerably due to Virgil's tantrum.

"Perhaps we could speak outside?" she asked Mr. Teedle. "We have some advice we'd like to ask you about Virgil."

"Certainly," the man said, setting his book aside. He stood and walked to the doorway, where he then waited with his fingers tapping his thigh while Henry struggled to turn the pram around and wrestle it back out into the hallway.

Rose cast a longing look around the Research Library before she followed them out. She had spent every spare moment she could in this room for years; that was how she had become acquainted with Mr. Teedle. When she had been in high school, this had involved a great deal of irritation on her father's part and a great deal of protests from her mother that they really would have liked to see her before six pm on Tuesdays through Thursdays.

This had never caused a jot of difference. Nor had starting college: she had simply spent what time she could here, and then gone home to complete her homework before starting dinner. Unlike her roommates, she had never been particularly interested in social activities, so she had felt no great loss in missing these.

But now, she had not been here once since Virgil had hatched, as it was a struggle merely to find time to do her homework and sleep. She had barely even come to the museum since then. With a pang of loss, Rose watched the door close, shutting her out of her favorite place in the city.

"What is it?" Mr. Teedle asked. "Are you wondering how much larger he will grow in the next month? We have some estimated charts based on his growth over the past eight weeks."

"No," Henry said. "Well, yes. That would be nice to know, but . . ."

"We have some *specific* concerns," Rose said. "Namely: what would you recommend as a long-term bed for Virgil? Somewhere that he cannot escape from as he gets older, and which would be both fireproof and safe for him?"

Mr. Teedle looked thoughtful. "Perhaps something made out of brick, like is used for a fireplace? My daughter-in-law has a wooden contraption called a playpen that she uses for their daughter. I wish those had been around when my children were babies. Something like that, only made out of brick, might be appropriate for Virgil."

Rose's heart soared. That was a truly useful idea!

"How fast could we get one made?" Henry asked.

"Well, I imagine you would need the permission of your landlord to install what would amount to a permanent piece of furniture," Mr. Teedle said. "But other than that, I believe the cement takes one or two days to dry? If you could find someone willing to sell you bricks and lay them tonight, it could be ready by Christmas."

"Perfect," Henry said. "Where could we go to buy bricks?"

And how much will it cost? Rose wondered. They had already spent a concerning amount on presents and the now-charcoaled tree. Despite Rose's vehement protests that it was unnecessary and a waste of money, Henry had gone out and bought Virgil several more stuffed animals.

Never mind that the only interest their dragon son seemed to have in the teddy bear Henry had bought him was to dig his claws into it and pull out stuffing.

Never mind that it had been singed twice from Virgil breathing fire on it.

Never mind that Virgil referred to it as "prey."

"Actually," Mr. Teedle said excitedly, "I believe that Mr. Jones is currently working as a bricklayer! If anyone can understand your situation, he will. I'm sure he would be happy to help!"

Rose tried not to show her dismay. While Harrison Jones was a friendly man, she was not particularly fond of him. He was rarely kempt, and his breath usually smelled quite unpleasant.

She glanced over at Henry, and he looked no more enthused than she felt. She suspected Henry's dislike of the man stemmed from the fact that he had allowed Violet to be kept in a zoo with no concerns or argument. She had chosen him to be her father, and then he had cheerfully turned around and handed her to the care of others who saw her as no more than an extremely precious, rare animal.

Still, necessities were necessities. It was true that Harrison Jones would likely be happy to help.

"How do we contact Mr. Jones?" Rose asked politely.

"I don't believe he has a phone," Mr. Teedle said, frowning. "At least, not of his own. He lives at a boarding house."

Of course he does, Rose thought. *What need has he for a fixed address when he can pay someone to do his housekeeping and keep his daughter inside a zoo?*

But perhaps that was unfair. After all, he had not planned to have a daughter: Violet had come into his life suddenly, just as Virgil had come into Rose and Henry's.

Perhaps he is making do the best he can, the same as we are, Rose thought.

"Ah! I know," Mr. Teedle said. "I know he visits Violet daily. Perhaps the best way to contact him would be to go to the zoo and wait until he comes to see her? I'm sure Virgil wouldn't mind playing with her while you're waiting, and I assume you two both have the week off school, so if you have no pressing other concerns . . ."

Henry cringed.

"We were just there," Rose said. "It did not end well. Virgil behaved quite abominably."

"And if we go back now, he'll think his tantrum convinced us to go back," Henry growled.

"I'm familiar with that challenge," Mr. Teedle chuckled.

"We can leave him a letter with our phone number to call," Rose decided. "Mr. Teedle, could we perhaps borrow a pen and a sheet of paper?"

"Of course," the man said.

Thirty minutes later, they were walking down 5th Avenue away from Central Park Zoo.

"Do you think those people ever worry about money?" Henry asked longingly, looking across the street at the abodes that had been built for the super-rich.

"I think probably most people worry about money," Rose said. "Whether or not they need to."

"It would be nice just to know our money won't run out before I graduate," Henry sighed, taking a hand off the pram to rub his forehead while he continued to push with the other. "Virgil's carnivorous diet is costing more than it should."

"Then perhaps," Rose hinted strongly, "he does not need a diet of stuffed animals to supplement it."

"You can't be stingy with a child at Christmas!" Henry said.

Rose snorted.

There was a wriggling in the pram.

Virgil liked that noise. He was going to snort, too. Snort, snort, snort —

"*No!*" Rose and Henry shouted, diving for the pram to grab their son before he set the whole thing ablaze.

CHAPTER 4
Charm

When they arrived back home, their landlord was waiting outside the door for them.

"Do you have something to tell me?" he demanded, his tone strongly implying that the correct answer was *yes*.

Henry swallowed. "Virgil burned down the Christmas tree last night. We caught it before it caused too much damage, but —"

"Oh, really?" the landlord asked heatedly. "Have you seen the carpet in there?"

"We apologize for the carpet," Rose said swiftly. "We are taking steps to make sure this will not happen again."

"I've told you tenants again and again, don't light the candles until Christmas Eve!" Mr. Torgerson fumed. "And don't leave them lit overnight!"

Henry looked startled.

Rose was taken aback.

"You've . . . experienced burning Christmas trees before?" Henry asked cautiously.

"I wish I could just ban them outright," the man huffed. "This is the third time something like this has happened in the past five years! But when I tried to ban Christmas trees last year, oh no, everyone called me Scrooge."

Rose bit back a chuckle. The man's first name was Ebenezer. She didn't think showing amusement at the nickname would improve their landlord's mood.

"Well, we're very sorry about the . . . candles," Henry said. "We'll make sure that won't . . . happen again."

"Of course it won't, because you are not lighting those candles again!" Mr. Torgerson said. "And you *will* pay for the carpet!"

Henry cringed.

What a jolly season, Rose thought. *I hope we will not be destitute by the time it's over.*

Virgil poked his head out of the pram, as if he had determined that this would be the best moment to make his presence known.

Could he eat now? He was hungry. Hungry, hungry, hungry. Where was his food?

"Right here," Henry said, walking into the kitchen. He opened up the icebox and pulled out a covered bowl that had cooked chicken meat, raw egg, and butter mushed together. He pulled the cloth off the top of the bowl and scooped up some of the mash with his hand.

Mr. Torgerson watched with evident curiosity. "Is that what a dragon eats?"

"Back in the Cretaceous Period, he would have eaten one of the prey species of dragons," Rose said. "We've found that bird meat is the closest approximation we can come to it."

Virgil wriggled his tail over the side of the pram, and then tumbled out. He landed on his head on the carpet.

Mr. Torgerson's eyes widened, and he looked about to lunge forward to see if the baby was all right.

Virgil rolled over onto his stomach, not seeming to notice the fall. He half-rolled, half-crawled across the floor to where Henry was waiting.

"OW!" Henry shouted as Virgil put one of his clawed hands onto his ankle. He reached down and unhooked the baby from his pant leg.

Virgil was hungry. Virgil wanted food. Virgil wanted to be fed by mouth.

"No, for the thousandth time, I'm not putting it in my mouth," Henry said. He leaned over and held out his hand.

Virgil's neck darted forward, and he snapped up the chicken and chewed busily. Sharp teeth glinted as it shot forward again.

Mr. Torgerson watched with awed apprehension. "Doesn't he bite you?" he asked.

"Thankfully, no," Henry said. "Which is more than I can say for some human children. My nephews, for instance."

The landlord chuckled nervously.

Rose decided that this might be the best time to speak up. "We'd like to build a brick bed for Virgil to sleep in," she said. "This would allow us to restore the oven to its original purpose. We will cover the cost, and it will eventually be a playpen, as well."

"Oh," Mr. Torgerson said, seeming too riveted watching the dragon to think much about the question. "Would it be, um . . . removable?"

"We could lay a layer of cardboard on the floor so that any cement drips on that, and nothing is affixed to the floor," Rose said.

"Hmm," the landlord said, his eyes on Virgil. "You know, when I first read what the paper said, I thought it was some kind of hoax or joke. And then I saw you two walk out with that thing . . ."

"Dragon," Henry said. "He is a dragon. Not a thing."

"You know, I'd love the chance to meet the other one," the landlord said. "Is it true they're both intelligent? Do they both talk like . . . that?"

Virgil was done eating, and now he wanted more food. The hand was empty! Where was his food?

Henry glanced down and reached into the bowl to scoop out more for Virgil.

"Both *Deinonychus* dragons are telepathic, yes," Rose said. "We believe it was a trait unique to their species, but we have no way to be sure. We're certainly glad it's the case, because there would be no other way to communicate with them."

"Bet it's quite an adjustment," the landlord said. "Eating chicken instead of stegosauruses, huh?"

Virgil didn't know what he meant. Why was the strange man thinking about bones?

"*Stegosaurus* lived in the late Jurassic Period," Rose said. "*Deinonychus* come from the early Cretaceous. They were approximately thirty-five million years apart. It's highly unlikely the two species ever met."

Virgil's father thought Virgil's mother was being pedantic again. Virgil didn't know what that meant. Why was Virgil's mother annoyed with Virgil's father?

The landlord coughed, as if trying to hide his amusement.

Rose smiled. *For once, Virgil has managed to be helpful. It seems the child has some charm.*

The little dragon raised his head, eyes bright with curiosity.

Virgil wanted to know what charm was. Hey! Virgil hadn't been done eating! Virgil's father shouldn't take the food away!

"We have your permission, then?" Rose asked rapidly, hoping that Virgil would not spoil the man's goodwill while they had it. "To build the bed for Virgil?"

"Hm?" the landlord asked. "Yes, I suppose so. As long as you cover the cost, and nothing is permanently altered." He glared in the direction of the oven, as if his gaze alone would remove the metal doorstop and nail affixed to it.

"Thank you," Rose said in relief.

The next half an hour was tense, as they waited for the landlord to leave, and he seemed to want to hover, watching Virgil with rapt interest.

Rose was terribly afraid that, at some random moment, their son would decide to snort, and sparks would fly from his nose. If he did that, the landlord might catch on that it hadn't been the candles that had burned down the tree, and his goodwill might transform to fear or hostility.

Then it occurred to her thinking about that might give Virgil the idea, so she tried to pull her mind away from the possibility. But that, of course, led inexorably back to it. So at last, she moved as far away from the kitchen as possible without being rude, and hoped that she was out of Virgil's range.

"What do you do for dinner?" the landlord asked curiously. "Seeing as your oven is not hooked up any longer?"

"We use our neighbors'," Rose said. "Speaking of which, I actually should go and start preparing that now . . ."

It was early yet, an hour before she normally would go next door and ask, but anything seemed better than sitting around here waiting for him to leave.

"Ah, yes," Mr. Torgerson said, standing. "Of course. My apologies for intruding. But no more lighting candles in here, no matter how traditional it is!" he added sternly.

"Yes, sir," Henry said, nodding quickly.

Rose nearly collapsed with relief on the couch as the door shut after the man. She put her head in her hands.

Henry walked over, carrying Virgil, and rubbed her shoulder. "I know," he said. "I'm glad we didn't get thrown out, too."

Virgil was sleepy. Virgil was tired. Virgil was soaking. Virgil was wet. Wet, wet, wet, wet, wet . . .

"Your turn," Henry said, holding up the dragon.

Rose sighed and collected the baby. The cloth pinned around his hindquarters and the top of his tail was, indeed, soaked through and smelly.

"Thank you for not breathing fire in front of the landlord," she murmured as she went to find a fresh one.

Virgil was too tired. Virgil was wet. Wet, wet, wet, wet . . .

CHAPTER 5
Chimney

Can't be done," Harrison Jones's voice said as soon as Rose picked up the phone.

"Excuse me?" Rose asked, breathing heavily.

She was trying not to pant. She had run to grab the phone before it could awaken Henry, seeing as he had decided to get an hour of sleep as soon as Virgil had settled down for a nap.

"Can't be done," Harrison repeated. It sounded like he was shrugging. "Not tonight, not tomorrow night, certainly not on Christmas. It might be possible to have someone do it in a month, if you wanted it done outside, but indoors? Maybe if you paid my company a lot, and I do mean a lot, of money, they'd be willing to take on such a major construction project, but you'd need the agreement of your landlord."

"But it's not a major project," Rose objected. "It's —"

"It *is* a major project," Harrison's voice said. "You're talking about designing something that doesn't currently exist, and which has no market outside yourselves."

"But it would be similar to a chimney!" Rose protested. "Or a playpen! Nothing complicated at all!"

"That's not what you said in your note," he retorted. "You said you wanted something he can't crawl out of. Whenever he starts climbing, I doubt he would find difficulties with a brick wall."

21

Rose said nothing. He was, appallingly, correct. If they wanted a bed that would keep their son penned in each night for longer than a few weeks or months, however long it took the little dragon to learn to climb, they would require something that would be safe, something that would be easy to deposit him into, and yet something that would be difficult for him to escape on his own. Her mind failed to imagine a shape which would accomplish all of these things.

"What you probably want is a cage," Harrison said. "You could ask the zoo what they'd recommend."

Rose said nothing. Her fist clenched around the phone. He was absolutely right: a cage would fit the parameters they'd defined, and the very idea was appalling. She had no doubt that Henry would veto it with vehement certainty.

Maybe we've been thinking with the wrong assumptions, Rose thought. *Maybe what we need is not to find a way to trap him, but a way to make sure it is not dangerous if he gets out on his own, which he will no doubt want to do increasingly more often as he ages.*

"Thank you, Mr. Jones," Rose said politely. "I appreciate the speed with which you contacted us."

"If you need to contact me again, here's the phone number for the boarding house," he said, and recited four digits. "I'm not often here, though. And it's often busy. There are three other boarding houses on our party line, plus at least two families, and one of the women in one of those places is constantly on the phone."

"Speaking of which!" a strange man's voice cut in. "Are you two close to done? I need to make a call soon."

Rose rubbed her forehead. That was a voice she thought she had heard before, so the rude stranger was probably on the end of her party line. It would have been nice to be able to hold a conversation without the risk of strangers listening in. The lack of privacy with telephone conversations was a definite disadvantage to using them.

"I believe we're done," Rose said, hiding her annoyance.

"Yup, we're done," Harrison agreed.

She hung up the phone, her mind unsettled. It seemed that she and Henry had, unknowingly, settled into the same mindset that had resulted in Violet's living situation. This was something that they must not do, not if they wished better for Virgil.

She walked over to the oven, where she peered in at Virgil. He was asleep with his tail curled around him, his back rising and falling in regular rhythm. As she watched, his tail twitched, and he let out a tiny sneeze. A spark escaped his nostrils.

Rose shut the door carefully, making sure it didn't clang as it hit the metal that kept it from closing completely. In the tiny gap, she could almost make out the outline of his growing-rapidly-more-ragged cloth diaper.

How do we do what is best for Virgil, and also best for us? Rose wondered.

She knew exactly how his birth parents would have handled it: they would have allowed the child free rein. But as Virgil aged, he would not be simply a toddler, he could be one which could set anything on fire, and yet who still probably needed exercise and freedom to develop.

A large cage, like Violet's, would probably work for a very young child quite admirably. But what about when their child aged? It didn't seem wise to set the precedent that ensnarement was the only reasonable option. They must find an alternative, and they must find it quickly.

Who might have an insight that might help? Rose wondered.

Then she realized. She realized that they had been going to the wrong experts for ideas.

She picked up the phone to ask the operator to connect her to her mother, and instead heard two strangers talking loudly, one of them the rude man who had interrupted her conversation earlier. It seemed to be an argument about in-laws visiting one of the strangers' homes.

Rose slammed the receiver back down. *This might not be a conversation I want to have over the phone, anyway! I will have to talk to my parents when we see them tomorrow.*

Tomorrow was Christmas Eve, and they would be going over for dinner; that had already been arranged. But if there would be no solution until then, Rose would need to come up with a stopgap that would work for tonight. One that would guarantee safety.

Rose thought about that for a long moment, and then moved one of the kitchen chairs against the oven door. That would stop it from opening for one night, at least.

She sat at the kitchen table in the other of the two chairs, and picked up her textbook. It was uncomfortable to have no homework to work on during the silent moments, as that left her with little to work on but darning the huge pile of worn-through socks of Henry's that had accumulated over the past two months, a necessity she found unutterably boring but which he seemed to assume was her duty.

She had, as such, already purchased three of the textbooks that she would need for next semester, and had spent all her spare time reading them. Perhaps if she allowed the socks to accumulate until he had no more left, he would make the effort to mend them himself, as he had before they'd been married.

It wasn't until she had memorized the contents of three pages that Rose looked up, somewhat disturbed. She stared at the oven and the chair pushed up against it. Her stare became fixed.

Isn't that solution inconsistent with the resolution I made? she wondered. *Isn't that stopgap measure once again a way to trap him?*

Rose yanked her thoughts away from the disturbing notion and went back to her textbook. But her focus was no longer with it. She kept looking up and staring at the chair, more and more bothered by it.

If there's a way I want to do something, I must start the way I intend to finish, she thought. *It doesn't do any good to immediately flout the ideals I wish to follow.*

She stood up and walked over to the oven. She pulled the chair away, and it scraped loudly against the tile floor. There was a rustling from inside the oven.

Virgil was awake! Virgil had had a good nap!

Rose opened the oven door and gathered the little dragon up in her arms.

"I'm sorry," she said. "I'm trying. I just don't know what to do."

Virgil wasn't sorry. Virgil didn't know why his mother was sorry. Virgil was fine. Virgil was — Virgil's stomach hurt!

Rose scrambled to tuck him back in the oven, but she wasn't in time. A roar from Virgil's nostrils hit the back of the chair, which ignited into a small flame. She beat it back with her elbow until the chair merely had a dark spot against the seat. She stared at the baby in frustration.

Virgil's stomach felt better now. Could Virgil roll on the floor that was soft?

Rose sighed deeply and moved him to the carpet. After that tremendous burst, he shouldn't need to breathe fire for another few hours. The need seemed to build up in him, much like releasing the results of his digestive system.

Virgil rolled around and sunk his claws into the carpet. Virgil liked the floor that was soft! It was soft and rolly!

"And I have no idea what we're going to do," Rose murmured. "Why can't you make things easy?"

CHAPTER 6
Chore

Henry looked very taken aback as he walked into the living room. "What . . . are you doing?"

"I am moving the couch cushions to the floor of the kitchen," Rose said, walking past him with the second of three. "Was that not evident?"

Henry followed her into the kitchen, stepping around Virgil, who was busily clawing one of the charred branches of their Christmas tree. "Why?"

"In order to sleep in the kitchen tonight," Rose said. She placed the second cushion in line with the first one and strode back to the living room.

Henry followed her. "Why?"

"So that, if Virgil decides to exit the oven tonight, he will land on top of me, which will awaken me, and he will therefore not roam around the apartment unsupervised." Rose gathered up the third cushion and moved back to the kitchen.

"Doesn't that seem a little convoluted?" Henry protested, trailing after her. "There has to be a better solution."

"I imagine there is," Rose agreed. She walked past him to reach the linen closet in the hallway. She pulled out their one and only spare sheet and tucked it under her arm, then headed back to the kitchen. "I hope my family will suggest it tomorrow night."

"I mean, there has to be a better solution *tonight*," Henry said. "Why don't we . . . uh . . ." He cast his eyes around the kitchen, then spied the chair that was out of place. "Why don't we put this in front of the oven door?" he asked triumphantly, seizing it.

"That would be lovely if we wished to keep our son in a cage," Rose said flatly.

Henry loosened his grip on the chair. "Huh?"

"Harrison Jones called while you were sleeping," Rose said, tucking the sheet around the couch cushions to make a rather unappealing facsimile of a mattress. "He informed me that what we had described to him was a cage. It occurred to me that if there is no functional difference between Violet's living situation and Virgil's, we might as well be putting him in the zoo and have done with it."

"Hang on," Henry said, grabbing her hand. "Rose, there's a world of difference between the two. For one thing, Virgil actually lives with us."

Rose shook his hand off. "Harrison Jones visits Violet."

"Yes — visits! That's a big difference!"

"Would you put a human infant in a cage?" Rose challenged.

"Yes!" Henry said. "That's what a crib *is*! It's a place to keep a human infant restrained!"

Rose stared at him flintily.

"Look," Henry said, "getting Virgil a safe place to sleep that won't put him or us at risk isn't a bad thing. It's good parenting."

"A cage is out of the question," Rose said.

They stared at each other for a moment, tension bristling between them.

"Fine," Henry said shortly. "Then at least let *me* sleep on the floor. You sleep on the bed."

"You are a sound sleeper," Rose shot back. "What guarantee is there that you'd waken if Virgil fell on you?"

"I woke up this morning," Henry said heatedly.

"One instance is not a guarantee!"

Virgil rolled across the carpet and stared at them from an upside-down, sprawling position.

Why were his parents angry? They should feed him. He was hungry. He wanted food.

Henry opened up the icebox and groaned. "I forgot. We're almost out of chicken. Can you buy one and get it cooked today?"

Today? Rose thought. *You only just woke up from your nap, and I have not yet caught up with my sleep from our interrupted morning!*

"I will ask my mother to purchase one for us tonight," Rose said, keeping her temper in check. "We can pay her back for it tomorrow. We could even ask her to cook it for us before we come."

"Do you have to lean on your mother for everything?" Henry exclaimed. "Do you know how to cook yourself? I haven't had a hot meal since we got married, except when we visit your parents!"

"Virgil . . . was sleeping . . . in the oven," Rose said coldly. "I was not going to impose upon our neighbors any more than necessary, given that sandwiches and such could suffice."

"Is that going to change when we get him a different bed?" Henry exclaimed. "Are you ever actually going to cook dinner? You haven't even darned one of my socks in six weeks!"

"You know how to darn them yourself," Rose snapped. "We're both in school. We're both equally busy."

"I shouldn't *have* to darn them!" Henry said. "It's your chore!"

"Oh, really?" Rose asked icily. "Why is that?"

"Because that's what wives do!"

"Well, perhaps husbands," Rose said coldly, "could make some effort at an equivalent number of chores."

"I take care of all the finances!"

"As I've said before, I wish you'd let me see them."

"I feed Virgil!"

"So do I."

"I change his diapers!"

"So do I."

"I wake up in the middle of the night to do both of those!"

"So do I."

Admittedly, that was far more than Rose's father had ever done, and perhaps Henry's father as well. So perhaps he wanted to be reminded that she appreciated that he didn't seem to think their son was all her problem. Rose opened her mouth.

"*And* I let you go to college!" Henry added.

Rose's mouth snapped shut.

"*Let* me?" she shouted once she had recovered from speechlessness. "*Let* me? In what way do you *let* me?"

For some reason, Henry seemed determined to not back down from the atrocious statement. "I talked your father into paying your tuition! I talked the dean of your college into letting you stay after we got married!"

Rose pursed her lips. Henry had had to go in and assure the dean that he did not mind if his wife continued her college education. To her intense displeasure, it had turned out that married women were not allowed to continue as students without special permission. That had enraged her.

For what possible reason had Henry brought up such a sore subject? To enrage her further?

Henry seemed to take her silence as agreement. "I know most men wouldn't accept their wives being in college. I *do!* I just ask that you take care of the things you're supposed to do!"

Rose clenched her fists and reminded herself that her father had said far worse. It had never helped to shout, though she had done it many times despite knowing that.

"I see," Rose said quietly. "It is good to know that that is where you stand. I will be sleeping in the kitchen tonight, and I will be glad of it."

She turned to walk through the living room to get her pillow, and nearly tripped over their son, who was lying on the carpet batting at one of the tree's charred bottom branches.

Were Virgil's parents mad at him? Could Virgil have food? Virgil was still hungry. Virgil was wet. Virgil's tail was in the wetness. It was uncomfortable. Could Virgil have food?

"Yes, you can have food," Rose said. "If we run out of chicken before tomorrow night, you can have eggs and butter alone."

Virgil liked chicken food. It was prey. One day his parents would teach him how to hunt prey. His father had given him prey, but it didn't taste good. Could he have his prey?

"No, you can't have your teddy bear right now," Henry said, sounding annoyed. "And yes, you can have food."

Virgil liked food! Virgil would roll over to his father! Now he was on the hard floor. The soft floor was more fun to play on. Was Virgil's mother tired? Was she taking a nap?

"Perhaps I should," Rose said. "I'm still short on sleep from this morning."

"Fine," Henry muttered. "Sleep as long as you want. It's not like I can't make sandwiches for myself."

It's not like the person who has the shorter commute to school can't learn to cook for himself, Rose thought.

But she didn't continue the argument. She just went to the bedroom, where she fell asleep almost as soon as her head hit the pillow.

Chapter 7
Choleric

Bad tempers abounded the next morning. Though it was Christmas Eve, neither Rose nor Henry made any effort to speak to each other. Rose spent most of the morning with her textbook, while Henry spent most of it absorbed in the small book where he kept an account of their finances. For some reason, he kept looking up and staring at Virgil quite often before going back to his pencil scribbling.

Virgil spent most of the morning rolling around on the carpet, sometimes clawing at the brown, dried needles that had fallen from the tree. At one point, one flipped into his open mouth, and Virgil's expressionless face somehow gave the impression of disgust and betrayal.

That was not-food! Why was not-food in his mouth? He didn't like it!

Rose and Henry both started to stand up, noticed the other standing, hesitated, and then Rose sat down and Henry got up to remove the foliage from their child's mouth.

They alternated feeding Virgil without discussion, this being an ingrained habit. They did run out of chicken by lunchtime, which Rose discovered when she got up to take her turn, so she cracked raw eggs into a pat of butter and fed that to Virgil, which he seemed very disgruntled about.

This was not-food! No, that was food. That was not-food! No, that was food. That was not-food! Virgil wanted his food!

Henry looked silently triumphant.

Rose tried to ignore this.

The phone rang several times, causing them to jump from their seats, but it was always the wrong sequence: one long ring and two short ones, three long ones, and one short ring and two long ones. That meant the phone was for another household. Rose hoped that none of these conversations lasted long enough that the call they were waiting for failed to come through, but given the frequency of the ringing, it seemed likely that the conversations were all of short duration.

At last the correct ring came, two short and one long, and Rose leapt from her seat to answer it.

"Hello?" she asked, hoping that it was her mother. Her family had agreed to call as soon as they felt Christmas dinner was only an hour away. It was barely two minutes past two, and Rose's mother had estimated dinner would start at four o'clock, so Rose would be overjoyed to leave this tense atmosphere to walk there early.

"Hello, Rose," her father's voice said on the other end of the phone. "Your mother says the chicken's ready, so if you want to come over early, you can. Your sisters are insisting they want to string popcorn, and your mother wants to go caroling as soon as we're done with dinner. You planning to come along?"

"That sounds delightful," Rose said. She did not consult with Henry. If he did not want to go, she would simply leave him behind at her parents' home.

"It looks like snow," her father added, "so you might want to wear your warmest coats."

"Understood," Rose said. "We will be over as soon as possible. We'll see you in an hour or so, Papa."

She set down the phone, and it immediately rang. She jumped, but it was only two long rings and one short one, meant for somebody else.

"They're ready early," she told Henry. "We can leave now."

"Hallelujah," he said, slapping his finance book shut as she passed. As usual, Rose resisted the urge to peek, but she wished he would not act like it contained some dreadful secret. It was rather unsettling.

A crash came from the direction of the Christmas tree, and Rose spun around. Virgil had just snapped off one of the branches at the bottom with his head as he raised it.

Were they going to see Violet? Could Virgil come play?

"We're not going to see her," Rose said. "We're going to see your grandparents. The zoo's not even open today."

Virgil was very disappointed. He wanted to lie down next to Violet and hit her with his tail. Then she would hit him with her tail and he would catch it in his claws. It was fun to play.

"I'm sure it is," Rose said, "but it's Christmas Eve, which is a special day that's all about family."

Virgil didn't know what that meant. Was Virgil's father going to breathe fire with him? Was Virgil's mother going to hit him with her tail?

"Virgil, as I've said a thousand times," Henry said wearily, "we're human. That means we're different species. We can't do the same things."

Virgil's parents were being mean! Virgil was pouting.

Rose turned away from the petulant baby and walked into the bedroom. She pulled on her warmest stockings, which were woollen and a trifle itchy, and then stared at the open drawer, pondering.

At last, she reached into the back and pulled out the luxury she had been saving, her last pair of silk stockings that had not developed terrible runs from Virgil's claws on her legs. If there were ever a time to treat oneself, it would be Christmas Eve.

She walked to the hall closet and removed her coat from the rack. She tucked the ball of stockings into the pocket of her coat before sliding it onto her arms. Purses were fashionable, but she was not fond of them, especially while walking. The one purse she owned had been singed by one of Virgil's many escapades, in any case.

Henry was already clad in his coat and waiting by the door with a rather impatient air. He had Virgil tucked under his arm.

"Are we not taking the pram?" Rose asked.

"It's snowing," Henry said shortly. "If it continues, I don't want to push it through mountains of slush on the way back."

Rose had to admit that was sensible.

They opened the door, and a burst of cold air blew in on them. Rose shivered and hunched into her coat. She ran back to the hall closet and returned with both her scarf and Henry's. She wound hers around her neck and tucked it into her coat.

"Would you like me to put it on you?" she asked Henry, holding his scarf up.

Rose glanced over at Virgil, who was staring at the rushing snow with little apparent interest. His tail swung back and forth, clearly unbothered by the temperature.

What would it take for any temperature to bother him? Rose wondered. *He seems unharmed by fire, and snow is also of little concern to him. Do* Deinonychus *dragons have any sensitivities?*

Perhaps she should have been glad that their little son seemed virtually invulnerable, but it troubled her. How had his species died out in the first place? They must have had some terrible weakness, and it worried her that she did not know what it was. Perhaps they had simply starved to death because they had lost their prey species? Virgil still seemed to need ten or more meals per day, which implied a very fast metabolism and a rate of growth which would be unsustainable without a great deal of prey.

I hope that we are adequate as parents, Rose thought nervously. *What if he requires far more food next year than we can possibly afford to give him?*

Already he had grown a foot longer than he had been when he'd hatched. Suppose it turned out that he outgrew their home long before they were able to move to a larger place?

No, Rose told herself. *Don't borrow trouble. We will figure something out, in that case.*

Chapter 7: Choleric

But as they stepped out into the freezing wind and blowing snow, she couldn't shake the feeling that the choleric disposition Henry had shown was because he was bothered by something similar. They had not, after all, figured out what to do about their child's firebreathing.

Rose bent her head as she walked against the wind beside her husband and son, burying her hands deep in her pockets. She could hardly wait until they reached her parents' home and she would be able to thaw her toes.

Chapter 8
Cheer

Mama, they're here!" Sara shouted from the doorway.

Rose shivered into her coat and wished her sister would move out of the way and allow them inside.

Rose's mother bustled up behind her. "Oh, you're covered in snow!" she cried. "Come in, come in! Dinner's almost ready. Do you want to sit by the fire?"

"Y-yes," Henry said, his teeth chattering.

Rose nodded, her breath bobbing in front of her face.

Virgil's tail swung unconcernedly. Virgil wanted to play with the soft white stuff. Could Virgil play?

"N-not right now," Henry said, his teeth chattering as he stepped into the house after Rose. "We need to warm up."

Virgil didn't understand. His parents' memories made no sense to him. Why did they think it was cold? What was cold? Also, could Virgil eat? He was hungry.

"Can I feed him, can I feed him, can I feed him?" Sara squealed. "He's so cute!"

Fortunately, Virgil now accepted food from people other than his parents.

"Go ahead," Rose said as Henry relinquished the dragon.

Sara pranced off with their son in her arms. Virgil wasn't cute. What was cute? Virgil was hungry. Where was his food?

Rose and Henry walked to the living room, where they ensconced themselves next to the fire. Despite the impropriety, Rose removed her stockings right there and laid them out beside the fire to dry. She allowed the fire to warm her bare feet.

Her father came into the room, smoking a pipe. The odor was overpowering.

"Hi, Rose," he said. "Hi, other one. Good journey?"

Henry bristled. "It was cold," he said shortly.

Rose wished he wouldn't show offense at being called "the other one." That was why her father did it. Though the man now tolerated Henry, he had decided upon their first meeting that he didn't like him, and took delight in continuing to remind Henry of that at every opportunity.

"Snow's really coming down," Rose's father agreed. "I wouldn't want to walk in that."

"I wish I hadn't had to, either," Henry muttered under his breath.

"He's so cute!" Sara squealed, wandering into the living room with Virgil cuddled in one arm and gobbling out of her other hand, which held the usual mixture of chicken, raw egg, butter, and some water. "Look at the way he eats!"

Virgil's head jerked forward, he chomped at a mouthful, and he swallowed. Then his head darted forward again. His tail swung excitedly behind him, almost in rhythm.

"Yes, he is," said Rose, though she was used to the sight.

Louise trailed in after Sara, looking furious. "It's not fair! It's my turn to hold him!" she protested.

"Is not!"

"Is too!"

"Is not!"

"Is too! And I'm older!"

"Only by nine months," Sara sniffed.

"Ten!"

"Nine!"

"Ten!"

Rose rubbed her forehead wearily. It was hard to believe her sisters were in high school. When they squabbled, it sounded like they were ten years younger. The two usually got along extremely well, but not when they both wanted something.

Henry squinted at them, as if trying to figure out which girl was which.

"You can have a turn after Sara is done, Louise," Rose said, to remind him.

Henry's face cleared. He looked relieved.

"Hey, other one," Rose's father said, gesturing at Henry with his pipe. "You planning to come over tomorrow too, for Christmas morning?"

"No," Henry said, looking irritated. "We're planning to spend that at home, together."

With a blackened Christmas tree we barely managed to prop back up, Rose thought, looking around the room at the paper chains and paper doll chains her sisters had strung up along the top of every window. *And no decorations. And no Christmas cake to eat for breakfast in the morning, because we have no way to cook things.*

Tomorrow would be her first Christmas away from her family, and being here tonight just reminded her of just how bare and spartan their own apartment seemed. Christmas Eve was something, but it was not the same as Christmas Day.

"Too bad," Rose's father said. "Be nice to have Rose here. And the dragon."

Henry bristled again.

Lips curled upwards as he tucked the pipe back into his mouth, Rose's father departed the room.

"All right, my turn now!" Louise shouted. "He's done eating!"

"He is not!" Sara snapped.

"He is so!" Louise cried, grabbing for Virgil.

"He is not!" Sara glared, yanking him away.

"Be careful with him!" Rose snapped, standing. "He's a baby, not a doll!"

Virgil's tail swung as he dug his claws into Sara's arm. Was there more food? He was still hungry. Was there more food?

"Ouch!" Sara shouted.

"Virgil, be careful with my sisters, too," Rose sighed.

"See? He's saying it's my turn now," Louise jumped in.

"Dinner's ready," Rose's mother called from the kitchen. "You two, stop squabbling and help me set the table."

"But . . ." Louise complained.

"I'm busy holding the dragon," Sara announced.

Henry stood up, scooped Virgil into his arms, and walked away from them.

"Hey!" both girls wailed.

Virgil was still hungry. Was there more food?

Rose herded her sisters out of the room towards the kitchen, where they each collected something to take out to the table. Their father was, as usual, seated at the table waiting for the meal to begin, without an ounce of helpfulness offered.

Henry joined them when the table was set, and sat down with Virgil complaining vehemently on his lap. Protests about hunger and his parents eating while he wasn't filled the room as Rose's mother attempted to say grace.

As she finished, Henry looked down at the baby with exasperation. "Are you, by any chance, still hungry?" he asked.

Yes! Virgil was still hungry! Virgil wanted more food! Virgil needed more food! Virgil was still hungry, hungry hungry! What was his father shoving at him?

"It's ham," Henry said, dangling a tiny slice in front of Virgil that he had removed from his plate. "Try it."

Virgil didn't want that not-food. Virgil wanted food.

"It *is* food," Henry said. "You should be able to eat it. I doubt your digestive tract is so delicate that the only thing you can eat is chicken. Try it."

Virgil didn't want that not-food! Virgil was very sad! Virgil was going to cry!

Hands flung up over ears all around the table.

An ear-splitting screech emanated from the tiny body on Henry's lap, long and loud and piercing. It went for what felt like an eternity before it halted briefly.

"Stop him!" Rose's father bellowed.

Virgil had been taking a breath. Now Virgil was going to scream again.

"Stop it," Henry said. "Don't —"

The shriek began again, rattling through both ears and minds.

Rose's mother leapt up from the table and ran to the kitchen. She came back with a bowl full of chicken mash and held it in front of Virgil's face. She mouthed something that was inaudible behind Virgil's scream.

The little dragon stopped.

"— what you want, dear?" Rose's mother finished.

Yes. That was what Virgil wanted. That was Virgil's food. This person was nicer than his father. Virgil's father was mean.

Virgil poked his head into the bowl and gulped rapidly, as if he had not just eaten another meal just as large as his usual repast.

I hope this does not mean he is overindulging, Rose thought. *I do not want to deal with complaints of a tummyache all evening.*

"Some Christmas cheer for you," Rose's mother cooed, gathering up Virgil as the little dragon continued gobbling.

Henry's jaw clenched. He looked exceptionally annoyed.

CHAPTER 9
Chill

Virgil must have eaten more than his weight in chicken that evening. He ate enough that Rose's sisters were each able to take another turn, and then Louise protested that Sara had held him twice while she had held him once as Virgil drowsed off to sleep.

Rose was a little worried. Why was Virgil eating so much? Was this a sign that he was sick? Or was he about to go through a tremendous growth spurt? While the latter might be preferable to the former, it would still not make their lives easier.

It was nearly nine o'clock before they were able to go caroling, and Rose's father stated outright that he had no interest in going.

"Neither do we," Henry said immediately. "We need to be getting back home."

Rose opened her mouth to protest that she wanted to join, but she closed it. Henry had dealt with a trying enough evening already. It would not be fair to force him to stay in her family's house alone with her father.

She pulled on her woollen stockings, realizing with embarrassment that she had forgotten all about her silk ones and had been bare-legged through the entire dinner, though at least she had remembered her shoes. She pulled her coat onto her arms and wrapped the scarf around her neck.

She kissed her family members goodbye, Louise while she was buttoning up her own coat and Sara while she was pulling on a scarf, and then headed with Henry to the door.

He pulled the handle downward and pushed.

The door didn't open.

Frowning, Henry tried again.

It still didn't budge.

"This door does open outwards, right?" Henry asked.

"Yes," Rose's mother said. "It used to open inward, but the door kept hitting my china cabinet, so we had the hinges switched. Try again."

Henry tried again, shoving all his weight against it. The door didn't budge.

"Did the lock break?" Louise asked.

"Oh, wow!" Sara shouted, moving a curtain aside to peer out the window. "You won't believe how much snow is out there!"

Rose bolted to the window and stared out in horror at the pristine winter blanket that stretched out before them. Gobs of snow still kept on falling, glittering and bouncing against the window as if trying to reach into the room.

"Woww," Louise breathed, joining them. "I've never seen so much before."

"There has to be over a foot," Rose's mother agreed.

Rose felt a vague sense of panic. How were they going to get home?

"The back door opens inward," Rose's father called from the living room. "You can go out that way. Or you can go out a window."

"In this blizzard?!" Rose's mother demanded. "Of course they're not going anywhere! I don't want them catching their death of cold! Just think of Virgil!"

Henry's arms clenched tighter around their son, who was fast asleep. "Virgil will be fine."

"*Your* health, then!" Rose's mother said. Her eyes had taken on a flinty, obstinate cast that Rose had rarely ever seen. "I don't want you catching a chill or freezing to death out there!"

Henry hesitated.

"He said they aren't staying for Christmas," Rose's father called from the living room. "Don't coddle them, Mabel. They can walk home if they want to. It'll only take a few extra hours."

That seemed to decide Henry.

"Thank you," he said stiffly. "We would be delighted to accept your hospitality."

Rose glanced into the living room and saw her father grinning. Apparently he had learned one of her mother's methods of persuading people.

"You two can sleep in Rose's old room," Rose's mother said, taking Louise's scarf and Sara's coat as they removed them. "Virgil can sleep in . . . does he need the oven?"

Rose glanced apprehensively over at Henry, who was giving her a nervous look. For once, it seemed they were of one mind.

"Virgil can sleep in the . . . uh . . . ." Henry said.

"Virgil can sleep in the bathtub," Rose said, as inspiration hit. "If we remove the towels and the cabinet, there should be nothing flammable in there."

And I'll sleep on the floor outside the bathroom door to make sure he doesn't escape, Rose thought.

"Flammable?" Rose's mother looked taken aback. "Why is that a concern?"

"Because he breathes fire," Henry said, as if this were obvious.

"Well . . . yes, but . . . ." Rose's mother looked taken aback. "Surely not in his sleep."

Rose and Henry began talking over each other.

"Sometimes sparks fly out of his nostrils —" Rose began.

"He burned down the Christmas tree —" Henry said.

"— even when he's asleep —"

"— if he wakes up on his own again, which is why —"

"— and that's why he has the oven in the first place —"

"— don't even feel safe —"

"— something better, but I don't want to trap him —"

Rose's mother listened to the garbled account with an increasingly perplexed look on her face.

"Is there a way to get him *not* to breathe fire?" she asked.

"*No*," Rose said in frustration. "It's a natural part of his biology. He releases some kind of flammable gas post-digestion, and when it's released, he ignites it automatically. He can no more stop production of this than a human infant could stop the production of urine."

"Or a dragon infant, for that matter," Henry muttered, glancing down at their son. Rose noticed that the arm of his coat beneath Virgil's diaper looked damp.

"That sounds a little like bed-wetting," Rose's mother said thoughtfully. "I've had some experience with that. Sara wet the bed until she was ten years old, and she sometimes then got out of bed and proceeded to dampen the hallway."

"*Mamaaaaaaaaaa!*" Sara squealed in humiliation.

"He's a little young for potty-training," Henry said defensively. "He just hatched two months ago."

"Perhaps so," Rose's mother agreed. "But this was almost a separate issue. Sara was already potty-trained."

Sara's face was scarlet, and she looked ready to hit somebody.

"So what did you do?" Henry asked.

"You might try having him breathe out all the fire he can right before bed," Rose's mother said. "It might not solve the problem entirely, but it might help. If he doesn't need to eat in the middle of the night anymore, it might even solve most of the problem."

Rose gaped at Henry. He looked as stunned as she felt.

Did we go to the wrong people for advice? Rose thought. *Instead of dragon experts, should we have gone to other parents?*

Perhaps this blizzard was not a curse. Perhaps this blizzard was a Christmas miracle. That might have been exactly the advice they needed.

"Let's try it tonight," Rose said. "We'll see if it makes any difference."

As if on cue, Virgil wriggled and his eyes opened. Were his parents thinking about him? Were they thinking they wanted him to breathe fire? He would do it. He knew how to make his nostrils snort. Snort, snort, snort . . .

Henry yelped and raced for the kitchen. Rose raced after him and flung open the oven door. Just on time, because a roar of flame escaped Virgil's nose and blasted against the back, longer and louder than she had ever seen before.

No doubt a product of the child eating so much extra dinner.

Rose looked back at the doorway, where her mother was watching with an open mouth.

"Yes, he does that," Rose said. "That's why we're concerned."

"Wait till I tell my friends about this," Louise breathed.

"Why didn't you do that in the fireplace?" Sara asked.

"Because they didn't think of it, because they don't have one," Louise informed her.

Virgil felt better now. His stomach didn't hurt anymore. Something else hurt now. It was his . . .

Henry yelped again and raced up the stairs for the bathroom.

"Where is he going now?" Louise demanded.

"To change Virgil's diaper, and perhaps his own clothes if he wasn't in time," Rose said wearily. "Virgil really did eat a *lot* of food. Excuse me while I go up to help."

CHAPTER 10
Choice

Rose woke up before anyone else, eyes wide open as she lay on the floor outside the bathroom door. She wasn't sure why she had woken up, and the pile of blankets on top of her was warm, while the air on her face felt bitter cold, so her eyes drifted shut again.

Hungry! So hungry! Virgil was hungry, hungry, hungry! He would share it with his mother! HUNGRY HUNGRY HUNGRY!

Rose's eyes flew open again as the terrible feeling slammed into her mind. It was painful and persistent, and impossible to ignore.

HUNGRY HUNGRY HUNGRY!

Did I oversleep? Rose thought blearily. She rubbed her eyes and reluctantly dragged herself out from under the blankets. Goosebumps immediately prickled all over her arms, so she picked up the two blankets and flung one around her shoulders like a cape, then pulled the other one around her waist and tucked it in at the top, like a skirt. It dragged on the floor as she walked, but that didn't matter.

"Wait patiently, Virgil," she mumbled, knowing he would catch her meaning whether he could hear her through the bathroom door or not. She shuffled down the hallway, away from the range of Virgil's telepathic wailing.

Why was the child so hungry now, right when it was extra cold and that made it especially inconvenient? It was like the way he had chosen to hatch on the day of their wedding. Virgil's timing was exceptional, and not in a preferable way.

She shuffled down the stairs and turned on the light in the kitchen. The clock on the mantel took her aback.

Four o'clock in the morning? It's four o'clock in the morning? He usually eats at midnight, and that keeps him content until six!

This was not a good precedent. He'd eaten half the chicken last night; at this rate, the rest would be gone by lunchtime. Even if a butcher's shop was open on Christmas Day, they had no way of leaving the house currently. And that chicken had been intended to last Virgil nearly a week.

Why is he so hungry? Rose thought in frustration. She pulled the chicken out of the icebox, discovered it was nearly frozen, and turned on the stove and placed it in a pan to thaw. Impervious to cold he might be, but the chicken had to be sufficiently soft, or he might choke on it.

Rose cut off a piece of the hard stick of butter and dropped it in the pan to warm up . . . and then she stopped.

Is he impervious to cold weather?

She had assumed he was, because he did not seem to be able to sense hot or cold. He also did not seem to get sick. But perhaps the change in temperature affected him in other ways.

Virgil's warm-blooded, Rose thought slowly. *Even if this had not been conclusively determined by researchers studying him and Violet, it would be obvious just by the fact that he stays warm even while out in the cold. He clearly regulates his own temperature. He keeps himself warm.*

Doing that requires energy. That's absolutely unavoidable. So what if . . .

Rose stared down at the pan, frowning, as the butter bubbled and the chicken began to simmer. She turned it over slightly so that another side could warm up.

What if the cold weather is what's causing this increased appetite? What if the increased appetite is what's causing him to wake up outside of his normal schedule? Eating more would also result in the creation of more flammable gas, which might have been useful for adult dragons if they used that to create fires to keep themselves warm, or to kill prey for extra food. But in the human era, with the advent of central heating and wooden homes, it's just dangerous . . .

It all fit together, and it was so obvious that she couldn't believe she hadn't seen it before.

Rose held the cold top of the chicken with one hand while she pried warm chunks off the bottom with a fork, then dropped them into a bowl. She poured the melted butter, which was now rather brown, out into the bowl, too. Then she added a cracked egg and about a tablespoon of water, and mixed them thoroughly.

By the time she brough the bowl upstairs, Virgil was in a terrible state, letting out the equivalent of a telepathic unending scream to anyone within range — which was, fortunately, nobody else. Rose opened the bathroom door and walked in, finding him sprawled across the bathtub and rolling one way and the other as if frantic to find some way to escape.

By the time she brought the bowl upstairs, Virgil was —

HUNGRY! HUNGRY HUNGRY HUNGRY!

"I know," Rose said. "I brought food."

HUNGRY HUNGRY HUNGRY! HUNGRY HUNGRY HUNGRY!

"Here," Rose said in exasperation, holding out the bowl in front of his face. "Here's food. Do you want it?"

Virgil's tail lashed out and whacked the bowl out of her hands. It toppled and spilled across his head.

Virgil opened his mouth in fury. He was very upset! He was angry! He was hungry! No one was feeding him! He was going to scr—

Rose snatched a shred of chicken and hastily shoved it into his open mouth.

Virgil shut his mouth. This was food in his mouth. This was food in his mouth. Yes. This was food.

Virgil wanted more food now.

Chapter 10: Choice

Rose fed him the rest of the bowl's contents, and before Virgil could gripe that he still wanted more, she removed the blanket from her shoulders and draped it on top of him.

Virgil was still hungry! Virgil wanted more food! Virgil was under something soft. It was like the soft floor. Why had Virgil's mother put the soft floor on him?

"We're going to test something out," Rose said. "We're going to see if wrapping you in blankets is sufficient. We have the option of putting you in a cage, but if this works, I think it is a much better choice."

Virgil didn't understand. The soft floor on top of him was soft. Maybe he would take a nap now.

Rose waited until Virgil's eyes were closed, his mind was no longer letting out quiet murmurs, and she saw no signs of sparks flying from his nose. Then she stood, rubbing her arms to stop the goosebumps, and headed to the hall closet to find another blanket. She was fairly certain there was at least one more that was not being used.

She started to make a bed for herself on the floor again, and then she stopped. She walked down the hallway and peered in at Henry sleeping, snoring softly.

I'm awake, Rose thought. *We're in a house with a working stove. I have no homework to do right now.*

She picked up the new blanket, wrapped it around her shoulders, and headed back down to the kitchen to make him a hot meal for Christmas.

Chapter 11
Cherished

In the morning, apologies made and Henry wildly enthusiastic about his breakfast, Rose gathered up Virgil from the bathtub, and the three of them headed downstairs to join her family.

"Do you think we could have him sleep in the bathtub at home, instead of the oven?" Henry asked excitedly. "If we did, could we reconnect the gas and have actual cooked food every day?"

Don't get ahead of yourself, Rose thought. *I still have homework most days, and a longer commute to school than you. If you start darning your own socks, we'll see.*

But that was a conversation they could have on another day. For now, it was Christmas.

She watched her family members open presents under the tree with some regret. All the presents she and Henry had bought for each other, and for Virgil, were back at the apartment. Virgil would not be getting his new stuffed animal prey today.

"Here!" Louise said, handing a lumpy package to Rose. "For you!"

Rose opened it. A terribly-knitted scarf was within. She fingered the holes and uneven stitches. "Thank you," she said, touched. "Did you make it yourself?"

"Nope, I made Sara do it for me," Louise said proudly.

"For you!" their mother told Sara, handing her a large box.

"Is it the new dress I asked for?!" Sara squealed, ripping it open.

"For you!" Rose's father declared.

Henry took the package, looking startled. "For . . . me?"

Rose's father nodded. "That's right. Bought it myself."

Henry opened the paper slowly. Inside was a package of expensive-looking cigars.

"I don't smoke," he said flatly.

Rose's father grinned.

"And I have a present for Virgil," Sara added, walking over with an oddly-shaped package in her hand. "Want to open it?"

Virgil was busy rolling around in the loud stuff. It was really fun.

"Come on, there's wrapping paper right here," Sara coaxed, holding the somewhat-tapered brown package out. "You can roll on the paper, or shred it, and even keep what's inside."

Virgil didn't know. He liked the loud stuff he had right now.

Sara walked over to Virgil and picked him up out of the pile of discarded brown wrapping paper, which was now looking more crinkled and shredded than ever. She placed the protesting, wriggling dragon on her lap.

"Here," Sara said, grabbing an end. "I'll help you. You pull it like this . . ."

Virgil didn't want to pull it. Virgil wanted to play in the loud stuff. Virgil tried to get down.

Sara caught him before he fell all the way off her lap. She held him with one arm while she unwrapped his present with the other. It was a shiny metal bucket with the handle removed.

"You see?" Sara said excitedly. "Look how much fun this'll be!"

Virgil ignored the bucket and clawed at the wrapping paper which was now all over her lap. He liked that there was now loud stuff to play with.

Sara leaned over and put the bucket on the ground. She picked up Virgil and deposited him in it.

"Um —" Rose began, alarmed.

Sara tipped the bucket onto its side and gave it a mighty shove. It rolled in an arc across the room and slammed into a wall.

"Virgil!" Henry shouted, jumping to his feet.

Virgil's head poked out of the bucket. That had been fast. That had been fun. Could Virgil do it again?

"Yes!" Sara shouted. "I knew he would like it!"

Rose rubbed her forehead. This wasn't a game she would have encouraged, but as Virgil seemed unharmed, she supposed she couldn't object. Not for now, anyway. She might hide the bucket when they got home.

Henry put his hand on top of hers, and Rose looked over at him. He smiled. She smiled, and leaned into his shoulder.

When they got home, they'd need to talk about whose responsibilities were actually whose. However sincere his apology had been this morning, he needed to be told that his assumptions did not match her reality. Still, there would no doubt be compromises that could be made.

If hot meals were what mattered to him, perhaps she could find time to do that daily if he took charge of the laundry. She would not mind giving up washing Virgil's disgusting diapers. If laundry was what mattered to him, he could take charge of the groceries. If groceries were what mattered to him, he could take Virgil's midnight feeding so that she could wake up an hour earlier and buy groceries before class. And no matter what, he could darn his own socks, thank you.

"You know what?" Henry murmured, squeezing her hand. "I think this wound up being a nice Christmas after all. I wasn't sure it would be."

Rose smiled and squeezed his hand back. They watched their son use his tail to shove himself off from the wall and roll in the bucket for a ways. They watched Louise chase after him and fight with Sara over who got to push the bucket next. They watched her father catch the bucket and then hold it hostage while Virgil protested his new lack of mobility.

I hope the next dragon to hatch will be as lucky, Rose thought. *I hope he or she will be as cherished.*

Of course, she did not know for certain that a third dragon would hatch. But she could hope so.

Chapter 11: Cherished

And on a beautiful Christmas morning, surrounded by family and a tree that was not charred and had not fallen over, hope seemed more than sufficient.

www.ingramcontent.com/pod-product-compliance
Lightning Source LLC
Chambersburg PA
CBHW021125070726
47591CB00013B/887